CW00925695

One Little Word

Joseph Coelho
&
Allison Colpoys

Frances Lincoln
First Editions

The Argument comes
from nowhere.
It sits huge and bloated
in the middle of the playground
between me and my best friend.

I don't know where it came from.
I don't know its name.
I think it's here because of us.
We **yelled,** and it came!

All the kids in the playground
give it funny looks.

I stick out my tongue,

my best friend
screws up his face,

and The Argument
does nothing but...

...GROW!

I call it a bad name,

my best friend
shouts a
bad word,

and The Argument does nothing but...

...GROW
SOME
MORE!!!

We play separately
on different sides of the playground.
It feels like we have never been so far apart
with The Argument stretched out between us,
scaly and hairy, spiky and mean.

For a little while I forget about it,
I tell the others...
"I don't care. It doesn't matter."

But I do care, and it matters a lot.
The Argument's paw lays over the slide,
spoiling our fun.

The Argument's tail winds
around the roundabout,
spoiling their fun.

The Argument's shadow
shudders over us,
and it is not fun!
And just like that
we all get mad...

every single one of us.

Ado rains
mountains,

Melanie
storms
thorns,

Abus spins
nightmares,

Maz
gusts
lava...

And my old best friend and I yell...
"You're not my best friend anymore."

The Argument grins and balloons, pushing up against Ado and Melanie, squashing Abus and Maz...

lifting me and my enemy
higher and higher,
as we shout and rage,
scream and fume
at the very top of

The Humoungous Argument.

I stand opposite my enemy,
my enemy stands opposite me and I...

PUSH HIM!

And everyone gasps!
And everyone is scared.

And as soon as I have done it,
I wish I hadn't.

I feel sad and angry,
mixed-up and confused.
And he...

PUSHES ME BACK!

The first tears come
    as sniffles
that we wipe
    from our cheeks.

The second tears came
    as streaks
        that drip
from our noses...

but the third tears
come gushing out
as all the bad feelings
come rushing out

big and blue,
bigger than our
little bodies
can hold.

Something new starts bubbling up inside me.
A soft little something
rolls up from my heart
and pops out of my mouth,
a tiny little...

"Sorry."

My best friend looks at it with wet eyes,
as a soft little something
rolls up from his heart
and pops out of his
mouth too.
Another little...

"Sorry."

We hold our Sorries in front of us,
They wiggle and giggle and dance and glow,
getting bigger and brighter, and as their
light shines down on The Argument,
The Argument...

...Shrinks.

Little by little
The Argument we made
gets smaller and smaller.
Its paw slinks away from the slide.

It's tail unwraps from
the roundabout.

It's cold, dark shadow, leaves us.

The
Argument
gets
tiny.

We crowd around on hands and knees
peering and squinting until it shys away to...

...nothing.

Very soon we can't remember
what it looked like,
or even why it came
in the first place.

My best friend looks at me,
I look at my best friend,
and we make up and...

...hug.

And it is the best hug ever.

Abus and Ado,
Melanie and Maz all join in
until we are all hugging
and giggling,
laughing and happy...

...happy that we all know how one little word can shrink an argument.

To all the little people who have learnt the power of a little word – JC

For dearest Jasper – AC

Text © 2023 Joseph Coelho. Illustrations © 2023 Allison Colpoys.
First published in 2023 by Frances Lincoln Children's Books, an imprint
of The Quarto Group, 1 Tryptich Place, London, SE1 9SH.
T (0)20 7700 6700 F (0)20 7700 8066
www.QuartoKnows.com
The right of Allison Colpoys to be identified as the illustrator and Joseph Coelho to be
identified as the author of this work has been asserted by them in accordance with the Copyright,
Designs and Patents Act, 1988 (United Kingdom).

ISBN 978-0-7112-7909-4
eISBN 978-0-7112-7913-1

Illustrated in ink and edited digitally
Designed by Zoë Tucker
Edited by Lucy Brownridge
Published by Peter Marley
Production by Dawn Cameron

Manufactured in Guangdong, China TT042023
1 3 5 7 9 8 6 4 2